# Jem's Wild Winter

# Books by Susan Marlow

**Circle C Beginnings**

*Andi's Pony Trouble*
*Andi's Indian Summer*
*Andi's Scary School Days*
*Andi's Fair Surprise*
*Andi's Lonely Little Foal*
*Andi's Circle C Christmas*

**Circle C Stepping Stones**

*Andi Saddles Up*
*Andi Under the Big Top*
*Andi Lassos Trouble*
*Andi to the Rescue*
*Andi Dreams of Gold*
*Andi Far from Home*

**Circle C Adventures**

*Andrea Carter and the Long Ride Home*
*Andrea Carter and the Dangerous Decision*
*Andrea Carter and the Family Secret*
*Andrea Carter and the San Francisco Smugglers*
*Andrea Carter and the Trouble with Treasure*
*Andrea Carter and the Price of Truth*

**Circle C Milestones**

*Thick as Thieves*
*Heartbreak Trail*
*The Last Ride*
*Courageous Love*
*Yosemite at Last: And Other Tales from Memory Creek Ranch*
*Stranger in the Glade: And More Tales from Memory Creek Ranch*

**Goldtown Beginnings**

*Jem Strikes Gold*
*Jem's Frog Fiasco*
*Jem and the Mystery Thief*
*Jem Digs Up Trouble*
*Jem and the Golden Reward*
*Jem's Wild Winter*

**Goldtown Adventures**

*Badge of Honor*
*Tunnel of Gold*
*Canyon of Danger*
*River of Peril*

# Jem's Wild Winter

**Susan K. Marlow**

**Illustrated by Okan Bülbül**

Published by Kregel Publications, a division of Kregel Inc., 2450 Oak Industrial Dr. NE, Grand Rapids, MI 49505.



**Library of Congress Cataloging-in-Publication Data**
Names: Marlow, Susan K., author. | Bülbül, Okan, illustrator.
Title: Jem's wild winter / Susan K. Marlow ; [Okan Bülbül]
Description: Grand Rapids, MI : Kregel Publications, [2020] | Series: Goldtown beginnings ; #6 | Audience: Ages 6–8.
Identifiers: LCCN 2020019560 (print) | LCCN 2020019561 (ebook)
Subjects: CYAC: Winter—Fiction. | Gold mines and mining—Fiction. | Family life—California—Fiction. | Christian life—Fiction. | California—History—1850–1950—Fiction.
Classification: LCC PZ7.M34528 Jem 2020 (print) | LCC PZ7.M34528 (ebook) | DDC [Fic]—dc23
LC record available at https://lccn.loc.gov/2020019560
LC ebook record available at https://lccn.loc.gov/2020019561

ISBN 978-0-8254-4630-6, print
ISBN 978-0-8254-7630-3, epub

Printed in the United States of America
23 24 25 26 27 28 29 / 5 4 3

# Contents

# New Words

**blacksmith**—a person who makes and repairs things using fire and iron

**bobcat**—a wild cat with a spotted coat and a short tail

**cougar**—another name for a mountain lion

**forty-niner**—a prospector in the California gold rush of 1849

**kindling**—small sticks or twigs used for starting a fire

**mothballs**—small white balls made of poison to keep moths from eating wool clothing

**musty**—having a stale, moldy, or damp smell

**potbelly stove**—a wood-burning stove with a round body

**provide**—to give or supply something that is needed

**rut**—a long, deep track made by wagon wheels

**tawny**—a yellowish-brown color

**trapline**—a series of traps to catch wild animals

**trunk**—a large chest used for storing things

CHAPTER 1

# A Chilly Morning

*Rattle, rattle . . . bang!*

"Shh," Mama whispered. "Don't wake the children."

Too late.

Jem opened his eyes. Except for a faint glow, everything was dark inside his family's tent.

Mama held a lantern in one hand. Her other hand clutched a blanket around her shoulders.

She was shivering.

Pa squatted in front of the potbelly stove. It stood in the middle of the tent.

Jem didn't like that stove. It took up too much space. It was always in the way.

Sometimes Jem bumped into the potbelly stove and tripped.

In the summertime, he often stubbed his bare toes against the stove's legs. *Ouch!*

More than once, Jem had asked Pa why that ol' stove had to take up so much room in their tent. Pa hardly ever lit it.

Now, Jem knew why the stove was there.

A cold chill sneaked under Jem's covers. He pulled the quilt over his head until just his eyes peeked out.

*Brrr!* Why was it so cold?

Holding the quilt close, Jem rolled onto his side and watched Pa light the stove. Tiny flames licked the wood shavings.

Pa blew into the stove until the kindling caught fire. Then he added larger pieces of wood.

Soon, the fire was snapping and crackling.

Pa closed the stove's small door and stood up. "That should take the chill off."

Jem sat up. "Is it morning yet?"

Icy air swirled around his body. He shivered and dove under the covers.

"Not yet," Mama answered. "Go back to sleep."

Jem's teeth began to chatter. "I c-can't. It's too c-cold."

Mama ducked into a dark corner of the tent. When she came back, she laid another quilt over Jem's cot.

It was a big quilt. Big enough to cover his little sister's cot too.

Jem rolled over and looked at Ellie. She was asleep. The banging and rattling had not woken her up.

*Lucky duck!* Ellie couldn't feel the cold if she was asleep.

Jem kept shivering. "I'm still cold."

"The stove will heat this place up in a hurry," Pa said. "But until then, I have an idea."

He walked to the tent flap and slipped under it. Where was Pa going?

Jem found out a minute later.

Something big and heavy jumped up on his cot.

"For goodness' sake, Matt," Mama whispered. "Did you have to bring him inside?"

Jem's eyes grew wide. "Nugget!"

"Shh!" Mama shot at Jem.

Even in the dim light, Jem knew Mama was not happy.

She kept talking. "He's wet and smelly and—"

"Nugget's not used to this weather," Pa said softly. "Besides, he's a better blanket than a dozen quilts."

Mama sighed. Jem knew she didn't agree, but she would go along with Pa anyway.

Pa and Mama always stuck together.

Jem was glad about that. It meant that for the first time ever, his dog could sleep on his bed.

Nugget inched his way closer to Jem's head. He didn't make a sound.

Neither did Jem.

Mama blew out the lamp, and she and Pa went back to bed.

The only light came from the small air holes in the stove's door.

Jem put his arm around Nugget and pulled him close. The dog's warm body was already heating him up.

*Swish, swish, swish.* Nugget's tail brushed against the quilt.

He licked Jem's cheek once. Twice. Then he settled down and let out a quiet doggy sigh.

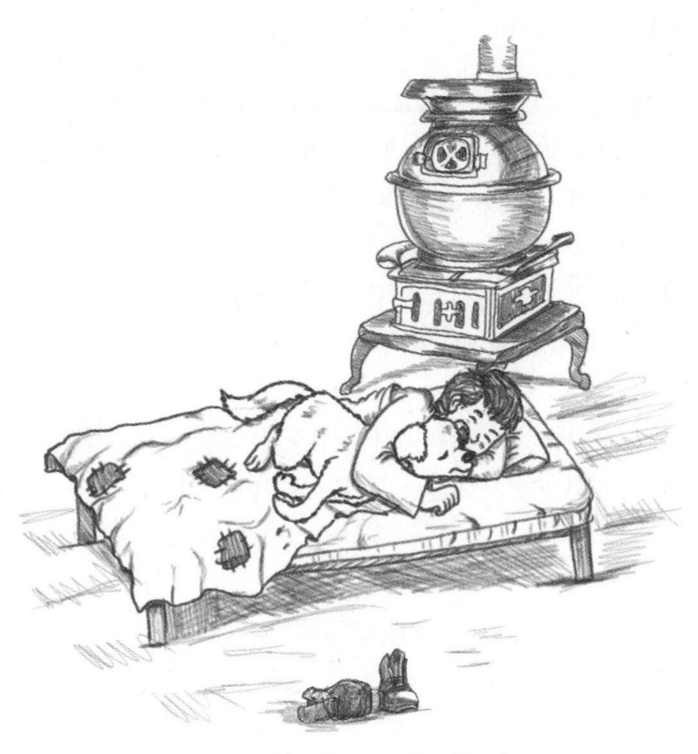

Jem stared at the firelight flickering through the air holes.

He was thinking hard.

Why would Pa and Mama let Nugget come inside in the middle of the night?

Jem listened. It wasn't raining.

Rain always made loud pattering sounds on the tent's canvas roof. Sometimes the raindrops were so noisy that Jem and Ellie couldn't hear each other talk.

Tonight, Jem didn't hear even *one* raindrop.

Besides, even when it rained, Nugget didn't come inside. He stayed dry under the outdoor table.

Sometimes he crawled under Mama's big outdoor cookstove to stay warm.

But on this cold night, Nugget was inside.

Jem yawned. Maybe it was too cold for even a furry dog to stay outside.

Pa added wood to the stove two more times before morning.

Jem woke up each time but fell right back to sleep.

The last time Jem woke up, the whole tent was warm.

He shoved Nugget off the cot, threw aside the quilts, and sat up. He stretched and yawned.

"Stay away from the stove," Mama warned. "It's hot."

It sure was. Jem smiled. It felt good.

Mama stood at the potbelly stove and stirred something in a pan. Next to the pan, coffee boiled.

What was going on?

Never in Jem's eight years had he seen

Mama cook inside their tent. She always cooked and baked outside.

"Why are you cooking on that little stove top?" he asked. "It barely holds anything."

Mama turned to Jem. "Go peek outside and you'll see why."

Jem jumped off his cot. Barefoot, he ran to the tent flap and yanked it aside.

A gust of cold wind hit his face. So did hundreds of icy white specks.

"Snow!"

## CHAPTER 2

# White Winter

Everywhere Jem looked, the world was white.

The tall pine trees were white. Their branches hung down, loaded with fluffy snow.

Mama's big cookstove was covered in white. Four inches at least!

And the snow was still coming down.

Jem's heart gave a happy thump. He had never seen so much snow.

Rain, yes. Buckets and buckets of rain. The rain sometimes lasted for days.

Last winter, Cripple Creek had risen higher and higher. Mama worried that the creek would run right inside the tent.

It almost did.

And the mud! Inches of sloppy, sticky mud.

Jem didn't like rain and mud. It was no fun panning for gold in a wild, rushing creek.

It was dangerous too. Mama never let Jem or Ellie go near the creek when it ran so high.

But snow?

There was only one word for snow. *Fun!*

Jem glanced around the gold claims. Campfires flickered. Miners were trying to keep warm.

It would be hard. Most miners along Cripple Creek didn't have potbelly stoves inside their tents.

Jem's friend Strike-it-rich Sam was one of those miners.

*I wonder if he's cold,* Jem thought.

Maybe Strike would like to sit inside the Coulters' tent and get warm. Or eat some breakfast.

Jem would ask him.

Quick as a wink, he dashed out of the tent. The snow burned Jem's bare feet.

He ran faster. "Strike!" he shouted.

The prospector raised a cup of steaming coffee. “Howdy, young’un.” He frowned. “Does your ma know you’re runnin’ around outside in nothin’ but your nightshirt?”

“No.” Jem found a spot near Strike’s campfire and sat down on a stump. He rubbed his hands. “I came to invite you inside our tent if you’re cold.”

"I ain't cold," Strike said. "I got this here fire."

The miner didn't look cold. He looked happy sitting next to his campfire and sipping coffee.

"Want a biscuit?" Strike peered at Jem's shivering body. "Or some hot coffee?"

Jem scooted closer to the heat. "No, thanks."

He lifted his cold, red feet to the fire. He couldn't stop shaking.

Strike chuckled. "Your ma's gonna skin you alive."

Strike was probably right about that.

Jem brushed the snow from his hair. It was melting fast next to the fire. "Have you ever seen so much snow?"

"Yep," Strike said. "Back in forty-nine. It was the first year of the gold rush."

"Really?" Jem's eyebrows went up.

Strike nodded. "I nearly froze to death. We forty-niners were taken by surprise."

Jem believed it. He sure had been surprised this morning!

"A bunch of miners left for the lowlands. The rest of us huddled together and shared food and campfires. We panned gold when we could."

Strike's voice grew sad. "A lot of miners died that winter."

"But not Pa and Mama," Jem said quickly.

"Of course not." Strike laughed. "Your folks had me to help 'em."

Jem let out a happy sigh. Strike-it-rich Sam was a good friend.

"A tent ain't the best place to stay warm and dry," Strike said. "'Specially when winter turns extra cold, like right now."

Jem nodded. He wished Pa would strike it rich so they could build a real house.

Maybe even a brick house like Will Sterling's, the richest kid in town.

Jem glanced back at his family's big tent. Most of the time, the roof and sides kept out the rain.

But would it keep out heavy snow? What if the roof ripped open from the weight?

What a terrible thought!

Jem watched Pa brush snow off the roof. He used a broom with a long handle.

It looked like Pa was worried about heavy snow too.

The only dry spot on the canvas roof was where the stovepipe poked through. The hot pipe melted any snow that tried to stick. Smoke curled up from it.

It looked warm and cozy.

That stovepipe looked scary too. Tents could burn down from a hot pipe, or from a fire in the stove.

Jem shivered. What if—

"Jeremiah Isaiah Coulter!"

Mama's shout sent Jem leaping to his feet. He tripped.

Strike caught Jem before he landed in the fire. "You're in trouble now, young'un. Better get on home."

"Are you sure you won't have breakfast with us?" Jem asked. He wanted to hear more tales about the forty-niners and the early gold-rush days.

"I've got these biscuits to eat." Strike popped one into his mouth. "Now get on home."

Jem jumped over the warm rocks and landed feet first in the snow. *Brrr!*

He ran as fast as he could, but the snow burned his feet worse than ever.

Mama met him at the tent door.

"For goodness' sake, Jeremiah," she scolded. "What got into you? You'll catch a chill for sure."

"I'm sorry, Mama." He ducked under the tent flap.

Heat hit Jem like a hot summer day. *Ahhh!* He sighed and sat down on his cot.

Mama handed him a bowl of mush and molasses.

"Thank you." Jem was mighty glad Pa had set up that potbelly stove.

*Yes, sirree!* He would never grumble about tripping over it again.

*Thank you, God, for a warm tent and good food,* Jem prayed quietly.

Then he dug into his breakfast.

CHAPTER 3

# What's in the Trunk?

"It's not fair!" Ellie gave Jem a grumpy look. She was sitting next to him on the cot.

"What's not fair?" Jem asked between mouthfuls of lumpy mush.

"You got to go outside in the snow." She crossed her arms and let out a big breath. "Mama won't let me."

"I didn't let your brother go outside either," Mama reminded Ellie. "He just went."

"I wanted to check on Strike," Jem said. "He might have been cold or hungry."

Jem wiggled his red, tingling toes. They were sure taking a long time to warm up.

"Strike-it-rich Sam can take care of

himself," Mama said. Then she smiled. "But it was kind of you to think of him."

Jem smiled back. Mama's scolding was over.

"But I want to go out in the snow too!" Ellie grumbled.

*Woof!* Nugget lay at the children's feet. *You don't want to go out in that cold white stuff,* he seemed to be saying.

Jem rubbed his feet in the dog's warm, golden fur.

Mama pointed to the tent flap. "Outside, Nugget. *Now.*"

Nugget rose and slunk under the flap.

"Mama!" Jem and Ellie shouted together.

She shook her head. "He can spend the cold nights inside, but not the day."

The tent flap opened, and Pa ducked inside.

So did a swirl of snowflakes.

Pa brushed off the snow and sat down on a cot. "It's mighty cold out there."

Mama handed Pa a cup of coffee. "This will warm you up."

Then Mama headed for a large trunk. She lifted the lid and dug through it.

Curious, Jem walked over. "What are you doing, Mama?"

"Looking for warm clothes."

When she stood up, Mama's arms were full of mittens, hats, and coats.

"We haven't used these things since the first year we came to the gold fields," she said. "I don't know why I kept them all."

Jem didn't know why either. The clothes smelled old and musty.

A sharp odor tickled his nose. "What's that awful smell?"

"Mothballs," Mama explained. "The clothes have been stored in this trunk a long time. Mothballs keep the bugs from eating them."

Jem sneezed and rubbed his nose. *Ugh!*

"Now, I'm glad I kept all these things," Mama was saying.

She looked up. "For goodness' sake, Jem. Change out of that nightshirt and into some warm clothes."

Jem obeyed in a hurry.

When he finished tying his boot laces, he warmed his hands at the stove.

Mama laid the nasty-smelling clothes on her bed. She lifted a pair of blue wool mittens.

"They're a little big," she told Jem, "but these should keep your hands warm."

Jem looked at the mittens thoughtfully. He remembered how cold his hands had been earlier.

Maybe stinky mittens were not so bad after all.

"Me too, Mama!" Ellie shouted.

Mama found hats, mittens, and warm coats for them both.

"Now I can go outside in the snow," Ellie said.

Jem whooped. "We'll stay warm." He couldn't wait to romp in the snow.

Mama clucked her tongue. "I hope this cold snap doesn't last long."

She handed Pa a heavy fur coat. "I'm not used to this much snow. How will I bake pies on Saturday?"

Jem stopped whooping. Ellie grew quiet.

Mama baked pies to sell to the miners. She baked pies to sell to the café in town.

Even rich Will Sterling's family bought Mama's pies.

Pa didn't pan much gold in the winter. It was too cold and rainy to squat next to a rocker box all day.

Mama's pies earned gold for the family in a different way.

But what if Mama couldn't bake pies in all this snow?

Pa laughed. "It's only Tuesday. The snow will melt away by Saturday."

He winked at Jem and Ellie. "You two better play outside while you can. Snow doesn't last long in California."

Mama gave Pa a long, scared look. "But what if it does?"

Jem's belly flip-flopped.

Maybe Mama was remembering that first winter. The winter Strike told Jem about this morning. The winter when the snow *didn't* go away.

And a lot of miners died.

Pa pulled Mama close. "Don't worry. I can always set my trapline. There's good money in furs."

Mama nodded but didn't say anything.

Jem's heart leaped. A fur-trapping line! Maybe Pa would take him along.

"Can I go with you, Pa?" Jem asked. "I went on that prospecting trip with Strike last summer. Remember?"

*Please say yes*, he begged silently.

Pa let go of Mama and ruffled Jem's hair. "I'll think about it, Son."

*I'll think about it* was almost the same as *yes*.

Jem was sure of it.

"But right now, I need your help." Pa looked at Ellie. "Yours too."

"What for, Pa?" Ellie asked.

"We're going to bundle up in these warm clothes and brush the snow off Mama's cookstove."

Mama smiled. "I do need something bigger than a potbelly stove to cook supper on."

"That's right." Pa kissed Mama's cheek. "Life goes on. I might even pan a little gold later."

Jem shivered. *Brrr!*

"Jem and Ellie can play in the snow today," Mama said. "But snow or no snow, they're going to school tomorrow."

*School?*

"Roasted rattlesnakes, Ellie!" Jem yelled. "Let's get that cookstove brushed off so we can play!"

CHAPTER 4

# Snowy School Days

Jem and Ellie played in the snow all morning.

The clothes Mama had found kept them warm and dry, even if they were a little too big.

Only Jem's toes grew icy. But an extra pair of wool socks warmed up his feet quick as a wink.

So did Strike's crackling campfire.

"A little snow can't get in my way," Strike told Jem and Ellie. "I'm off to pan for gold."

Jem's miner friend was wrapped in a bear skin. A furry hat covered his head. Rabbit-fur mittens hid his hands.

Strike looked funny. Like a fat grizzly bear.

Ellie wrinkled her eyebrows. "How can you pan for gold in those mittens?"

Strike laughed. "That's *my* worry, young'un."

He picked up his gold pan and headed for Cripple Creek.

Jem shivered. "He's crazy."

"Is Pa crazy too?" Ellie pointed. "Look."

Jem squinted to see between the snowflakes. Pa had joined Strike at the icy creek. They were brushing snow off the rocker box.

"Yep." Jem nodded. "Even Pa is a little crazy today."

Jem liked to pan for gold when the sun shone hot and bright. He liked to feel the cool water on his hands and feet.

Jem was not a rainy-day miner. Or a snowy-day miner.

Ellie giggled suddenly. "Nugget sure likes the snow."

Wagging his tail, Nugget pounced on snow mounds. He ate snow and rolled in it.

He barked. *Come and play!*

Jem left Strike's warm fire and chased Nugget. He threw snowballs.

Nugget ran after them. When he skidded to a stop, snow flew everywhere.

Jem and Ellie laughed and laughed.

• ★★★ •

Jem was *not* laughing the next morning. It was a school day.

More snow had fallen during the night.

Instead of playing in the new snow, Jem and Ellie headed for Goldtown.

*Crunch, crunch, crunch.*

Jem's boots tramped through the deep snow. It came up past his knees.

Ellie held Jem's hand and stepped in his footprints.

By the time they reached town, Jem was panting. "Walking in the snow is sure not as much fun as playing in it."

But the snow had stopped falling. At least for now.

He dragged Ellie along. "Hurry up, or we'll be late."

Miss Cheney did not like it when the children were tardy.

Sometimes Jem's friend Cole came to school late. He spent the first half hour in the corner on those days.

Jem didn't want to stand in the corner this morning. He wanted to sit down and rest.

But Ellie could not go faster. "I'm tired." She tripped and fell.

Jem yanked her up. He wanted to yell at her, but he didn't.

It wasn't Ellie's fault the snow was deep.

"We're almost there," he said in a kind, big-brother voice.

Jem looked around. A gray cloud hung over Goldtown. Smoke rose from dozens of stovepipes.

His belly flip-flopped. So many fires! Would the town burn down again?

It had burned down last winter, when it wasn't even this cold. No snow, either.

Most of the wooden buildings had burned. The tents too. Only the brick buildings had escaped.

Will's brick house stood just down the street. Smoke puffed up from its chimney.

Ellie sighed. "It must be nice and warm in a real house. I bet Maybelle never gets cold, even at night."

"Who cares?" Jem kicked the snow. "At least we have a stove in our tent. Cole doesn't."

Ellie didn't say anything.

"Cole likes coming to school on cold days," Jem said as they clomped up the school steps. "School is warmer than a campfire or a tent."

Even a tent with a potbelly stove.

The schoolroom *was* warm. Jem slid into his seat to rest. *At last!*

Miss Cheney was patient and kind all day.

She didn't send Cole to the corner when he came in late. She didn't send any of the tardy children to the corner.

"It's hard to walk in the snow," she said with a smile.

The rest of the school day went even better.

The children played in the snow during recess. They warmed up inside the schoolroom.

Miss Cheney even heated hot cocoa for everyone.

Jem had never tasted anything so good!

"What did Miss Cheney call that drink?" Ellie asked on their way home.

"Cocoa." Jem licked his lips. "It's mighty good."

"It sure is," Ellie said. "Maybe Pa can buy—"

"Watch out!" Jem pulled Ellie back.

Five deer leaped out in front of the children and dashed away.

Ellie yelped.

Three more deer sprang across the road and then darted into the dark forest.

Jem's heart pounded. *Where did all those deer come from?*

"Let's go." Shaking, he grabbed Ellie's hand. "It's getting dark. I think it's going to snow again."

Jem walked fast. He didn't like the dark clouds. He didn't like deer jumping out at him.

"Why were those deer running so fast?" Ellie asked. "What scared them?"

"I don't know. Maybe a—"

Jem stopped talking. It was not a good idea to scare Ellie.

It was not a good idea to scare himself.

"What?" Ellie asked. "Tell me."

"It was nothing." Jem swallowed. "Just a bunch of scaredy-cat deer."

He hoped.

## CHAPTER 5

# Pa's Great Idea

On Saturday, the snow was still there. It had not melted like Pa said it would.

The gray sky promised even more snow.

Pa panned for gold first thing in the morning. Jem went with him.

The rocker box rattled and clacked.

Jem shivered and watched.

Pa found only a few tiny nuggets. His fingers shook so much that Jem helped by picking up the gold with a tweezers.

It was slow, cold work.

"There are warmer ways to make money," Pa told Jem.

"How, Pa?"

Pa winked. "You'll see." He waved

good-bye to Strike and headed back to their tent.

Jem plodded along behind. What was Pa thinking?

"Is fur trapping your idea?" Jem asked.

"No." Pa laughed. "Walking miles in the snow to check traps doesn't sound warm to me."

Jem sighed. Too bad.

Then a different idea popped into his head. A scary idea.

There was only one place where miners could work and stay warm.

A place warmer than panning for gold in an icy creek. A place warmer than setting a trapline.

The new Midas mine up on Belle Hill.

It never rained underground. It didn't snow, either.

Jem's heart raced. "You're not going to work in the Midas mine, are you?"

A gold mine was dangerous. What if the candlelight went out? What if the mine caved in?

What if—

Pa stopped in his tracks. "Never, Son. I'd freeze first."

He took Jem's hand and squeezed it. "You don't have to worry about that."

Jem's thumping heart slowed down. He squeezed Pa's hand back.

*Thank You, God,* Jem prayed silently.

Pa put his idea to work as soon as they got home.

He and Mama lifted the outdoor table. They carried it inside the tent.

"You can roll out pie crusts without snow getting in the way," Pa said, smiling.

"You'll stay warm, Mama," Jem added.

Ellie clapped her hands. "I can help Mama make the pies."

Jem looked around the crowded tent. There wasn't much else to do in here.

Not now. There was barely enough room to walk.

Pa lit the big cookstove outside.

A roaring fire melted the fresh snow on top. Smoke poured out of the stovepipe.

"I have another idea," Pa said. "But it will take me all morning."

"Can I help?" Jem was bursting to know Pa's idea.

Pa nodded. "You can keep Mama's fire going."

Jem slumped and kicked a snow mound. "But—"

"I have to go to town," Pa explained. "I need you to look after the fire while I'm gone."

Jem cheered right up. "Yes, sir!" He would be the man of the family.

At least until Pa got back.

Jem stayed close to the cookstove all morning. It was toasty warm.

He watched the fire. He shoved wood into the stove's hungry mouth.

Sometimes, he threw a stick to Nugget.

But Jem did not leave his post.

Back and forth Mama went. She slid dried-apple and blueberry pies into the stove's oven.

She pulled crusty, sweet-smelling pies out.

By noon, ten pies sat cooling on the table inside the tent. A pot of beans simmered outside on the big cookstove.

Pa came home a few minutes later. He was pulling something big.

Jem and Ellie pushed aside the tent flap and peeked out.

"What's that?" Jem asked.

"A sled," Pa answered. "A big one. Big enough to hold Mama's pies."

Jem looked at Ellie. For once, she didn't say a word.

Pa laughed. "Did you think you were going to deliver pies with the wagon?"

Jem didn't know *what* to think. He hadn't

thought about how the pies would get to town.

But Pa had. "A wagon's no good in deep snow."

After lunch, Pa and Mama loaded the pies onto the new wooden sled.

It had metal runners and a long leather strap for pulling. "Tom helped me build it in his blacksmith shop," Pa said.

"It will do nicely," Mama said. She spread a clean cloth over the pies.

"Sims at the café wants four more pies today," Pa told her. "His customers like yours best."

Mama smiled. "I'll rest a bit and then roll out some more crusts."

Jem couldn't wait to pull the sled.

He put on his warm coat. He pulled his hat down almost to his eyes. Then his mittens went on.

"I'm ready. Hurry, Ellie!"

"Take it easy," Pa warned. "Don't hurry. This sled is not like the wagon. If you aren't careful, the pies will slide right off."

"Yes, Pa." Jem picked up the leather loop and gently pulled.

He smiled. A sled full of pies was much easier to pull than a wagonload of pies.

This would be his easiest pie delivery ever. He was sure of it.

Even if he had to be extra careful to not spill the pies.

## CHAPTER 6

# Scary Snow Days

The sled slipped along the packed-down trail like a quiet whisper.

It didn't bump over rocks like the pie wagon always did. It didn't fall into any ruts.

For once, Ellie did not have to hang on to the sides to keep the load steady.

"Yippee!" She kicked snow and played with Nugget all the way to town.

Nugget kept Will away from Jem and Ellie's pie deliveries. That mean rich boy never picked on them anymore.

Will did not even answer when Jem rang the bell at the Sterlings' big brick house.

The maid opened the door.

Will's little sister Maybelle peeked around the maid. "Hi, Ellie."

"Hi, Maybelle."

Will glared at Jem through the window. He made an ugly face.

"Pie peddlers!" he mouthed.

"Scaredy-cat!" Jem mouthed back.

The maid paid Jem and took the pie.

"Thank you." Jem had to pull off his too-big mittens to drop the coins into Mama's small pouch.

He worked fast. He didn't like hanging around Will Sterling's house.

Even if Ellie did.

Right now, she was trying to peek inside. She inched her way closer and closer to the open doorway.

"Ellie!" Jem grabbed her hand. "Let's go. We have work to do."

Ellie let out a big breath and followed Jem back to the sled.

The rest of the pie deliveries took no time at all. It seemed like every miner in town saw Jem's pie sled coming.

Soon, all the pies were sold. Mama's pouch was filling up fast.

Jem's heart gave a happy skip. "Maybe there will be enough gold to buy a small tin of—"

"Cocoa!" Ellie yelled. She jumped up and down.

Jem nodded. "Maybe."

He pulled the sled. It felt light as a feather. "Want a ride?"

"Yes!" Ellie plopped down on the sled and held on tight. "Go fast, Jem!"

For once, Jem was not afraid of tipping Ellie over. If she fell off, she wouldn't get hurt. She would land in the soft snow.

So, Jem ran fast. The sled flew behind him. Ellie shrieked with delight.

Nugget raced beside Jem, barking. His tail wagged.

Jem ran until his breath came in loud gasps. Then he pulled Ellie slower and slower.

Finally, he stopped. "It's your turn to pull the sled."

Ellie jumped off and grabbed the leather strap. "You can ride now."

For the first time ever, Ellie could pull her big brother. "You're easy as pie to pull."

"Building a sled was Pa's best idea ever." Jem closed his eyes and lay back.

*Grrr!*

Jem's eyes flew open at Nugget's low growl. His dog stood frozen in place.

Ellie stopped short. The sled bumped into her legs. "Ouch!"

"Shh!" Jem sat up and listened.

The forest on both sides of the road was quiet.

*Grrr!* The fur on the back of Nugget's neck went up.

"What's wrong?" Ellie asked in a scared voice.

Loud cackling and gobbling suddenly filled the air.

Jem let out the breath he'd been holding. "It's just turkeys."

He laughed. "Don't you dare go after those birds, Nugget."

Nugget might not obey Jem. His dog loved to chase wild turkeys. So far, though, he had never caught one.

Nugget growled again.

Jem grabbed his dog around the neck. "No, Nugget!"

Just then, a dozen turkeys raced out of the forest. They flew up into the air.

A tawny-colored mountain lion leaped after them. Giant paws swiped at the birds. Feathers flew.

The turkeys flapped their wings and flew higher.

The big cat landed in the snow on all four feet. He had a feather in his mouth, but no turkey.

Nugget barked, growled, and barked again.

Jem held Nugget tighter. "Please, God. Make the cat go away," he whispered.

The mountain lion took one look at Nugget and darted toward the woods.

Before Jem could blink, the cat was gone.

*Thank you, God,* Jem prayed silently. *That sure was a fast answer.*

Ellie started crying. "I wanna go home!"

Jem wanted to go home too. He stood up, and his legs felt wobbly. His hands shook.

"Get on the sled," he snapped.

Ellie didn't move. She kept crying.

Jem wanted to yell. He wanted to yank her down onto the sled.

But he didn't. A big brother didn't act mean when his little sister was really and truly scared.

Instead, he gently set Ellie on the sled. "Stop crying and hold on. Nugget won't let that ol' cougar get you."

Ellie rubbed her eyes and did what Jem told her.

Jem pulled the sled past the turkey feathers that lay scattered on the snowy trail.

He picked up the biggest one and handed it to Ellie. "Here."

She smiled and stuffed it inside her coat.

Jem passed the cougar's paw prints in the snow. He stopped and stared.

The prints were big. Four inches at least.

"Wait till Pa and Mama hear about this!"

Jem sucked in a breath and ran all the way home.

## CHAPTER 7

# Trapline

"Maammaa!"

Ellie's shriek echoed through the gold claim.

Mama shut the oven door and stood up straight.

Pa jumped up from where he was feeding the stove more wood. "Ellianna!"

Even Strike turned his head. He sat on a stump near the stove, drinking coffee.

Jem gave the sled one more yank and fell into Pa's arms. "It was a big cat, Pa!"

He talked fast, before Ellie could tell the story. "It chased the turkeys but didn't catch any."

"A bobcat?" Mama asked.

"A mountain lion," Ellie blurted. She threw herself into Mama's arms and started crying.

Mama gasped and held Ellie tight. Her face turned white.

Jem finished the story. "Nugget barked and growled, and the cat ran off."

Pa's hug felt extra good. "Thank you, God," he prayed, "for keeping our children safe."

"A mountain lion?" Strike shook his head. "Haven't heard of a big cat around here for years. They like to stay up in the high country."

Pa brushed the snow off a stump and sat down. He pulled Jem onto his lap.

Jem rested against Pa's chest.

Pa's heart went *thump, thump, thump*. Slow and steady.

Which meant Pa wasn't worried about the mountain lion.

"It must be all this snow and cold," Pa said. "Jem saw a small herd of deer the other day. Something was after them."

"When the deer come down to look for food, the cats follow," Strike said. "They gotta eat too."

Mama blinked back tears. “It’s a long way to town, Matt. That cougar could have snatched the children.”

“The Lord looked after them,” Pa said softly. “And Nugget did too.”

Mama blinked harder. “They’re not going to town alone anymore. Not even to school.”

No school?

Jem grinned. *Hurrah for the mountain lion!*

Mama sniffed. “Not until the snow melts

and the wild beasts go back where they belong."

Tears dripped down her cheeks. She wiped them away with her apron.

Jem's eyebrows went up. Mama sounded tired and scared.

Not like her usual self.

Mama never acted scared when the family went blueberry picking. Jem had even seen a black bear last fall.

Mama had seen it too. "It's minding its own business. We're minding ours."

And that was that.

So, why would Mama cry about a mountain lion? The big cat had been minding its own business too.

Maybe baking pies in all this snow and cold was too much work. Maybe Mama needed a rest.

Pa set Jem down and went to Mama. He shooed Ellie away.

"I'll take the last load of pies to town this afternoon," he told her.

Mama nodded and rested her head on Pa's shoulder.

"I can walk the kids to school too,"

Pa said. "You don't need to worry about them."

Jem slumped. He would rather stay home.

Pa's next words cheered Jem right up.

"I have an idea." He and Mama sat down on a big stump. "Why don't you rest from baking pies until the weather changes?"

Mama's eyes opened wide. "We need the money."

"I know." Pa nodded. "But I can set a trapline. Furs bring more money than pies."

"Matt's right about that," Strike said with a chuckle. "Fox, mink, rabbit. Maybe even a bobcat."

Tingles raced up and down Jem's arms. *Please take me!*

He knew better than to interrupt. Strike was still talking.

"I know you don't like Matt trapping far away, Ellen, but there are good spots close by."

Pa rubbed Mama's back. "This cold weather has brought the animals down to us. I could set a trapline above Cripple Falls and be home the next day."

*Please say yes, Mama!* Jem pleaded with his whole heart.

Mama didn't say yes. She didn't say no. She sat quietly and looked at her lap.

Jem sat quietly too. So did Ellie and Strike and Pa.

Everybody waited while Mama thought it over.

The cookstove hissed when snowflakes landed on it.

Water dripped from the edges. The sloppy mud in front of the stove steamed. Gray smoke puffed out of the stovepipe.

Mama let out a long, slow breath. "I don't like it, but I guess you're right."

*Yippee!* Jem could hardly sit still.

"Baking pies in this freezing weather is hard work," Mama said, shivering. "I do need a rest."

Pa rose. "I'll find my traps and get them ready."

Jem leaped up. "Can—I mean *may*—I go with you, Pa?"

"Absolutely not," Mama said. "Not with a mountain lion prowling around."

"But Pa said he would think about it." He grabbed Pa's hand. "Remember? You told me—"

"Jeremiah," Pa warned quietly. "Don't upset your mother."

When Pa called Jem by his full name, he meant business.

Jem ducked his head and sat back down. *No fair!*

Strike slapped his knee and stood up. "I feel like a snowy hike myself. Want some company?"

Pa grinned. "I'd like that a lot."

Jem rubbed his watery eyes. No crying!

Pa bent down close to Jem. "You take care of Mama while Strike and I are gone."

"Yes, Pa."

"I told you I would think about it," Pa whispered in Jem's ear. "And I will."

## CHAPTER 8

# Yes or No?

Pa left first thing Monday morning. He was gone all day. He was gone all night too.

Jem took care of Mama and Ellie.

He filled the wood box. He fed the chickens in their snowy coop.

Mama even let Jem light the potbelly stove when it went out.

Best of all, Jem did not have to go to school on Monday. He didn't have to go the next day, either.

More snow came down that morning. Jem and Ellie played outside.

*Woof! Woof!* Nugget shook off the snow and raced toward the creek.

Jem looked up from the snowman he and Ellie were making. "Pa!"

He took off running after Nugget.

Pa grabbed Jem and threw him up in the air.

Strike-it-rich Sam did the same thing to Ellie. She squealed.

"Did you set the traps?" Jem asked when Pa set him down. "Did you catch anything? Where are the furs?"

He peeked behind Pa's back. No furs there.

No furs on Strike's back either.

"Not so fast, Son." Pa laughed. "I just set the traps yesterday. I'll go back tomorrow or the next day to check them."

"Fur trapping is not a hurry-up kind of work, young'un," Strike added with a chuckle.

Jem grabbed Pa's hand. "Will you take me when you go back?"

"Wait and see."

Jem let out a big breath. He didn't want to wait and see. He wanted to know right now.

But Pa was firm. "Be patient."

Jem had no choice but to obey. He nodded.

Pa invited Strike inside their tent. "Share a hot meal with us."

When their miner friend agreed, he and Pa moved the big table back outside. It took up too much room in the tent.

Besides, Mama didn't need it anymore. Not until the cold weather was over.

Pa was all smiles during lunch. "We saw animal tracks everywhere."

"They're close by," Strike said. "Fox and mink. Even some beaver and bobcat."

"I could trap enough furs to keep us the rest of the winter," Pa said. "Before the critters head back to the high country."

He winked at Mama. "You wouldn't have to wear yourself out baking pies."

Mama smiled, but her eyes looked worried. "Did you see any sign of a cougar?"

"Not a track," Pa said.

Jem's heart leaped. He could not "wait and see" one minute longer.

"Mama, may I please go with Pa to check the traps?" His words came out in a rush.

Pa chuckled. "It's safe, Ellen."

Mama didn't say a word.

"It's only half a day's walk to the trap-line," Pa went on. "We might not even have to spend the night."

"Spending the night in the wilderness is not my worry," Mama said.

"It shouldn't be," Strike said. "We spend every night in the wilderness already."

Jem laughed. Strike was right about that.

Goldtown might not be part of the wilderness, but the gold claims along Cripple Creek were.

Just last fall, Jem had spent a night in the woods. Just he and Nugget.

Not on purpose. But Jem had been so tired that he had fallen asleep.

And before that, he and Strike had gone on a prospecting trip. Lots of nights in the wilderness.

"Strike and I set the traps so I can find each one quickly," Pa was saying.

Jem opened his mouth to ask again.

*"Be patient."* Pa's words spun around inside Jem's head.

He snapped his mouth shut.

"It's so cold," Mama said at last. "It was

different when Jem went off with Strike last summer."

"Jem plays outdoors all day in this cold," Pa said. "A snowy hike won't hurt him."

A thrill went through Jem. Pa wanted him to come!

Would Mama agree?

For once, Jem wished Pa and Mama didn't stick together so much.

"The trip will be good for him," Pa said. "We probably won't see snow and cold like this for another ten years."

"I certainly hope not," Mama said.

Pa grinned at Jem. "He can learn about fur trapping without going up to the high country."

Mama chewed on her lip. It looked like she was thinking hard. "That's true."

"I'll help out here while you're gone," Strike told Pa.

Pa nodded his thanks.

Jem held his breath. *Please, please, please,* he prayed silently.

"All right," Mama said at last. "So long as you think it's safe."

"It's safer than walking to town these days," Pa said.

Mama nodded. "You're right about that."

"Yippee!" Jem jumped so high that his fingers almost touched the canvas ceiling.

He and Pa were going on an adventure!

## CHAPTER 9

# A Snowy Adventure

Ellie jumped up and down. "Hurrah, hurrah!"

Jem stopped short. *Oh, no!*

Did Ellie think she was coming? She'd been too little to go on last summer's prospecting trip.

Would Mama let her go now on such a long, snowy hike?

"I'll help you get ready, Jem," Ellie said, smiling.

Jem's mouth fell open. "You don't want to go?"

"No!" Ellie looked at Jem with wide eyes. "I'll stay home and help Mama."

Pa tugged one of Ellie's short, dark-red braids. "That's my girl."

Ellie beamed.

Jem wrinkled his eyebrows. Why did Ellie want to stay home? She never liked being left behind.

The answer hit Jem like a splash of cold water.

Ellie loved animals. All kinds. Even tarantulas and mice.

She would not want to see a trapline. Not in a million years.

A new thought sneaked into Jem's head. Did he really want to see a trapline? He liked animals too.

Jem sighed. Too late now.

Besides, Mama looked so tired. Selling furs would give her a break from baking pies in this cold weather.

*I love Mama more than I like animals*, Jem decided.

He relaxed. Pa knew what he was doing, so it must be all right.

Jem didn't have time to think about the trapline the rest of the day. He was too busy getting ready to go.

Mama found him another pair of long johns. She also packed a warm sweater and an extra pair of wool socks.

"Just in case your feet get wet," she told him.

*Don't fuss so much, Mama,* Jem thought. *I'll be fine.*

But he didn't say those words out loud. He might hurt Mama's feelings.

Jem helped Pa load supplies. It was not the same as loading Canary with gold-panning supplies.

For one thing, Pa was not taking Strike's stubborn donkey.

*No, sirree!*

Pa loaded the new sled with a small canvas tent, warm bedrolls, an ax, and wood for a fire.

Mama packed a burlap sack full of jerky, biscuits, and a jar of cold beans and molasses.

*Yum!* Jem's stomach rumbled.

Ellie laid a canteen on top of the big bundle. Mama added cooking supplies.

Finally, Pa tied his rifle to the sled. "We'll leave first thing tomorrow morning," he said.

And they did.

· ★★★ ·

Jem and Pa hiked through the snow all morning.

First, they hiked along Cripple Creek. That part was easy. The snow was not deep.

Soon, the trail went higher. The snow got deeper.

Pa followed the snowy path he and Strike had tramped down on their first trip. The sled slipped along behind Pa.

Jem followed behind the sled.

The snow was not deep, but the air was cold. An icy breeze blew down from the mountains.

Jem wiggled his fingers. Even inside the mittens, his hands felt cold.

*Brrr!* He shivered and pulled his hat down over his forehead.

Pa finally stopped. "It's noon, and I'm as hungry as a grizzly bear."

Jem looked up. Gray clouds hid the winter sun. "How can you tell it's noon?"

"My belly is shouting the time," Pa said, laughing.

Jem laughed too.

Pa built a small fire to keep their hands warm while they ate.

The beans and molasses were icy cold. The biscuits were hard, but Pa heated some water.

Jem made a face. "Soaked biscuits don't taste very good."

"They'll fill your belly, Son," Pa said.

They didn't spend much time eating. Pa packed up, put out the fire, and started up the trail.

Soon, Jem heard a loud rushing sound.

Pa pointed. "It's Cripple Falls. We're almost to my trapline."

Jem watched the noisy waterfall tumble down, down, down into the creek below.

In a month or two, the weather would turn warm and sunny. Melted snow would fill Cripple Creek to the banks.

Miners would line up along the creek to pan gold.

*Me too!* Jem sighed. He couldn't wait for spring!

Pa shook Jem's shoulder. "Let's go."

The rest of the afternoon, Jem helped Pa check the traps.

Some were empty.

Other traps gave Pa a fox and a mink.

Pa was a good trapper. He knew exactly what to do.

When he held up a rabbit and yelled "supper," Jem grinned.

Roasted rabbit would taste ten times better than cold beans and molasses.

On and on they went. Pa found three more mink and two beavers.

He wrapped them up and added them to the sled.

Jem felt sorry for the animals, but he knew his family needed money.

"I'm glad Ellie's not here," he said.

"So am I," Pa said. "This work is hard on me too, Son. But God has provided these furs. They are worth a lot of money."

"Mama will be happy," Jem said. "Will we go home today?"

Pa looked up at the dark, cloudy sky. "If the traps were empty, we could have made it home in one day. But not now."

Jem shivered. "I hope we'll have a fire."

"We will," Pa promised. "And a hot meal."

CHAPTER 10

# Angels All Around

Jem sat wrapped in a blanket. His belly was full of roasted rabbit and hot beans.

The campfire flickered red and orange. He watched the sparks shoot up.

The clouds had blown away. Ten thousand stars twinkled in the cold night sky.

It was a perfect evening.

Later, Jem curled up beside Pa inside their small tent.

The wind started to blow.

The tent sides flapped, but Jem wasn't cold. He closed his eyes and fell asleep.

But not for long.

A low, terrible scream woke Jem up with a start. He gasped.

Pa's warm hand covered Jem's mouth. "Shhh."

Another scream. Louder this time.

Jem whimpered. The noise was coming from right outside their tent.

Pa wrapped Jem in his arms and held him close. "Don't make a sound," he whispered.

The moans and screams sent icy chills up and down Jem's neck.

He opened his eyes. It was pitch black, like the bottom of a deep coyote hole.

Only, if Jem looked up from inside a coyote hole, he could see the sky.

Not here. Not in this tiny tent in the middle of the wilderness.

Who was screaming? Who was moaning? Was it a crazy mountain man? Way up here?

He asked Pa in a whisper.

"It's a mountain lion," Pa whispered back. "He's prowling around outside our tent."

A mountain lion? Jem's heart pounded.

"He probably smells our catch," Pa said. "But I hung everything high out of any animal's reach."

Jem shook. *I want to go home!*

He couldn't. Not now.

"The cat won't come inside," Pa said. "I tied the tent closed."

Jem wasn't sure about that. A mountain lion had big claws. It could rip through a canvas tent with one swipe.

"Can you shoot it?" Jem asked.

"Not in the dark. We're safer if we stay still."

"I'm s-scared," Jem whispered. Hot tears stung his eyes.

"God is with us."

Jem didn't say anything. He couldn't. His throat was tight with tears.

Pa whispered a Bible verse in Jem's ear. "What time I am afraid, I will trust in thee."

The verse helped a little, but Jem kept shaking.

The mountain lion kept screaming.

Pa prayed. Then he whispered another Bible verse. "For he shall give his angels charge over thee."

Angels all around. Maybe ten thousand, like the stars Jem had seen earlier that evening.

He stopped shivering.

But Jem's heart kept beating hard and fast. It would not slow down.

Much, much later, the growling stopped. The big cat's screams grew quieter.

"The mountain lion didn't find what he wanted," Pa whispered. "He's going away."

At last!

Pa let out a long, slow breath. "Thank you, God, for sending your angels to protect us tonight."

He squeezed Jem. "We sure have a story to tell Mama, Ellie, and Strike when we get home."

Jem nodded, but he still couldn't speak.

Later, when Pa's soft snores filled the tent, Jem knew he was really and truly safe.

He fell asleep dreaming about bright and shining angels.

Thousands of them.

* ★ ★ ★ *

Pa untied the tent strings the next morning and poked his head out. He whistled.

Jem crawled up beside him. "What, Pa?"

"Take a look at these paw prints."

Jem pulled on his boots, hat, and

mittens. Then he pushed past the tent flap and stood up.

He sucked in a breath. Paw prints were everywhere.

The cougar had paced around their tent dozens of times.

Jem shivered. "I never want to hear another mountain lion scream."

It was the scariest sound in the whole world.

"Neither do I," Pa agreed. "That's the closest I ever plan to come to one of those cats."

He took down the animals he'd trapped and tied them to the sled. "Let's go home. The quicker the better."

To make the trip even faster, Jem sat on the sled with the furs and other supplies.

Sometimes Pa ran. The sled whizzed downhill.

Jem held on tight.

Soon, Jem saw their gold claims.

Mama and Strike sat around Strike's campfire drinking coffee.

Ellie was playing in the snow with Nugget.

Jem jumped off the sled before it stopped. He had never felt happier to be home.

"Mama! Ellie!" he yelled. "Just wait till you hear how God took care of Pa and me last night!"

# A Peek into the Past: Fur Trapping

The first fur trappers in our country were Native Americans. They caught animals for food and clothing, and to trade.

Native Americans taught the early explorers how to trap. They also traded furs for beads, pots, axes, and cloth.

Trappers caught all kinds of animals—mink, fox, bobcat, otter, and more. The furs from these animals were used for clothing.

The most valuable fur during the 1600s to 1800s came from beavers. Beaver fur was used to make the top hats men liked to wear. The fur could also be made into many other hat shapes.

Beaver hats were popular for many years.

Trapping animals for fur is not popular today. Many traps are cruel and dangerous. Other materials, such as wool and cloth made from cotton, can be used instead of furs in these modern times.

But for Jem and his family in 1860, fur trapping was a way to have warm clothing. It was also a good way to earn money.

* ★ ★ ★ *

Download free coloring pages and learning activities at GoldtownAdventures.com.